Mahina
and Koa the Gecko

Tenajah Naeʻole-Turner

WestBow Press books may be ordered through booksellers or by contacting:

WestBow Press
A Division of Thomas Nelson & Zondervan
1663 Liberty Drive
Bloomington, IN 47403
www.westbowpress.com
1 (866) 928-1240

ISBN: 978-1-5127-8402-2 (sc)
ISBN: 978-1-5127-8401-5 (e)

Library of Congress Control Number: 2017905849

Print information available on the last page.

WestBow Press rev. date: 06/15/2017

WESTBOW
PRESS®
A DIVISION OF THOMAS NELSON
& ZONDERVAN

Dedicated to my Grandmother Diane

Special Thanks to my mom for all her
love and support and to Kela Strickland
for bringing the characters to life.

It was a beautiful summer day in Hawaii and Mahina was visiting her Tutu. Mahina loved to discover new things and put them in her little bag of discoveries to show her Tutu.

Mahina looked inside a small hole in the garden post and saw something that looked like a white pebble. She picked it up and put it in her bag of discoveries.

"Aloha Mahina!" Tutu said.

"Aloha Tutu!" Mahina replied.

"What are we going to do today?" Mahina asked.

"Today we're going to the beach. I am going to pick ogo and you can look for seashells," Tutu said.

"What is ogo?" Mahina asked curiously.

"Ogo is seaweed that we eat and it is very yummy," Tutu said smiling.

And Tutu and Mahina walked down to the beach.

Down at the beach, Mahina looked for seashells and Tutu looked for ogo.

"Is this a seashell Tutu?" Mahina asked.

"No, not that one Mahina that is a rock," Tutu replied.

"Look here Mahina this is what I am looking for," and she picked up a handful of ogo and showed it to Mahina.

Mahina thought it looked like a spider with many legs.
Mahina and Tutu continued to walk along the beach.

"I wish I could find a seashell," Mahina said sadly.

"I'm sure you will Mahina. You just have to be patient and keep searching," Tutu said cheerfully.

Mahina searched everywhere for a seashell. She looked in the tide pools, under seaweed, under rocks, and in the sand. Still Mahina didn't find any seashells. Each time Mahina thought she found a shell, she would hurry to her Tutu and ask her, "Is this a seashell Tutu?" and each time Tutu would shake her head saying no.

Mahina was feeling very discouraged. She looked down at her toes and started to cry. Mahina felt silly for crying.

Clearing the tears from her eyes, she saw something hidden in the sand under seaweed and picked it up.

Mahina carefully examined it in her hand. Finally, Mahina walked over to her Tutu and asked one more time. "Is this one a seashell Tutu?" Mahina asked hopeful.

Mahina was so happy she finally found her very own seashell. Mahina gently placed the shell in her bag of discoveries.

After a wonderful morning at the beach, Mahina and her Tutu headed back to the house. Mahina took her discoveries out of her bag and put them on the kitchen table. Something was happening. The white pebble began to move!

"Tutu look! My pebble is breaking!" Mahina exclaimed.

"Oh Mahina, that is no pebble. That is a mo'o, a little gecko and it's hatching," so Tutu and Mahina watched the mo'o hatch.

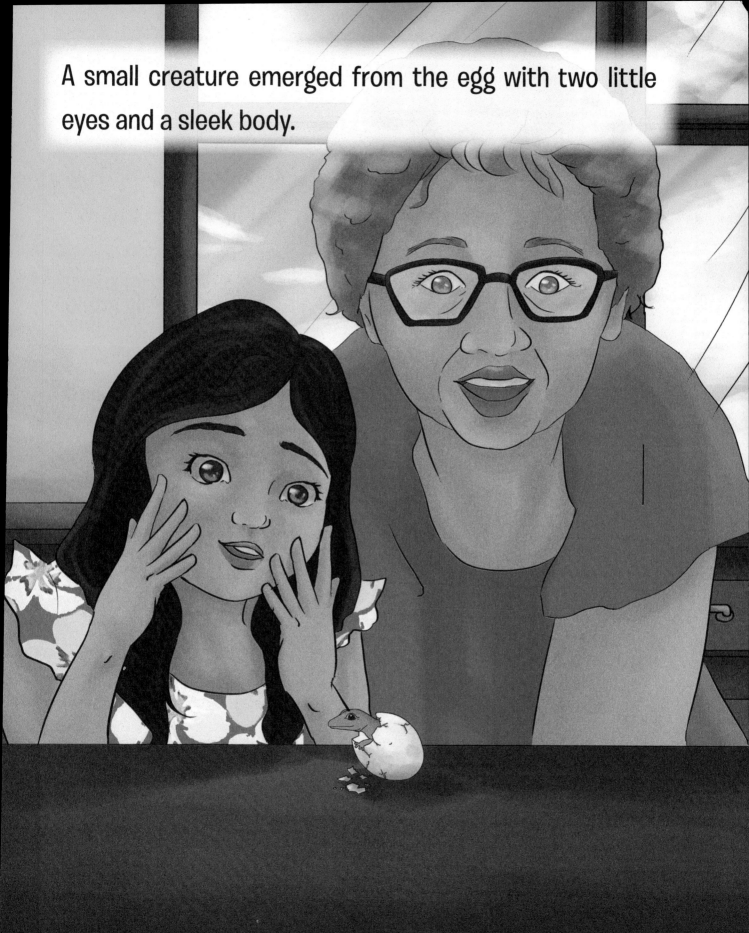

A small creature emerged from the egg with two little eyes and a sleek body.

"Oh! Can we name him Tutu?" Mahina asked pleading.

"Okay dear, what would you like to call him?" Tutu asked.

"How about Koa the mo'o?" Mahina said with a big smile on her face.

"That sounds like a lovely name, Mahina," Tutu replied with a smile of her own.

"Oh no, he's running away!" Mahina yelled.

"That's okay sweetie, he'll find his way outside," replied Tutu cheerfully.

That morning, Mahina and Tutu had banana pancakes and orange juice for breakfast. Afterwards, Tutu told Mahina which of her discoveries were pieces of coral and which were pebbles. When Mahina and Tutu were cleaning off the kitchen table. All of a sudden, the mo'o leaped upon the orange juice glass and licked the straw with his little pink tongue.

"Tutu look, Koa is back! And he's drinking my orange juice!"
Mahina squealed.

"Oh my goodness! Shoo! Shoo!" Tutu said waving her arms at Koa as he scurried off behind the microwave on the counter.

"I hope Koa will find his way outside so he can make friends with the other geckos," Tutu said as she cleaned up the kitchen table.

Later that day, when Mahina was chasing butterflies outside, Koa peeked from the microwave and saw Tutu washing the dishes and humming a tune.

"Aloha Koa, don't fall in the water," Tutu said cautiously.

Tutu watched Koa climb the wall to her ceiling as he playfully moved from the kitchen to other parts of the house. That night, Mahina asked Tutu to read her a bedtime story. As they were reading, Koa climbed closer to them to listen to the story too.

"Look Tutu!" Mahina said, as she pointed to where Koa was on the ceiling. "He wants to listen to the story too," she said.

"I think you're right Mahina. I'm sure by tonight he will also find his way outside," Tutu said as she tucked Mahina into bed.

Mahina let out a big yawn and stretched. As Tutu finished the story, Mahina fell right to sleep. Koa yawned too and climbed down the ceiling and fell asleep on the pillow next to Mahina.

"Good night Mahina, sleep tight," Tutu said.

Tutu smiled at Koa as he slept on the pillow and scooped him up with her hands and gently took him outside and placed him on her mango tree in the back yard.

"Good night Koa, sleep tight." Tutu said and walked back to the house and turned off the porch light.

THE END

Glossary

Hawaiian words and names

Aloha	Hello, goodbye, love
Mo'o	lizard or reptile of any kind
Koa	Brave
Mahina	Moonlight
Tutu	Informal name for grandmother
Ogo	seaweed in Japanese

CPSIA information can be obtained
at www.ICGtesting.com
Printed in the USA
LVOW05s1914241017
553641LV00026B/81/P